Hanna's
Cold
Winter

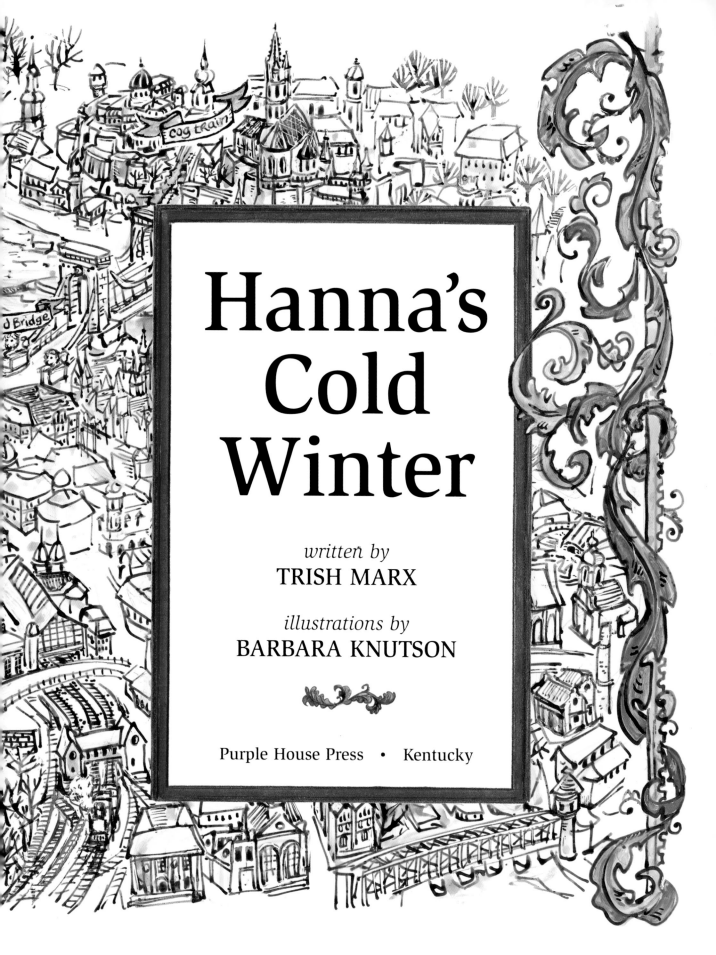

Hanna's Cold Winter

written by
TRISH MARX

illustrations by
BARBARA KNUTSON

Purple House Press • Kentucky

The author wishes to thank Tibor Fülopp; The American-Hungarian Library, New York; John Otterpohl; Suad McCoy.

*To Patrick, Molly, Annie, Jody and Court,
who helped me visit the hippos*—T.M.
To Thandi, who likes hippos—B.K.

Publisher's Cataloging-in-Publication Data
Marx, Trish.
Hanna's cold winter / by Trish Marx; illustrations by Barbara Knutson.
p. cm.
SUMMARY: A child tells how his family and other people in Budapest help save the famous hippopotamuses in their city's zoo from starving one difficult winter during World War II. Based on a true story.
1. World War, 1939-1945—Hungary—Budapest—Juvenile fiction.
[1. World War, 1939-1945—Hungary—Budapest—Fiction. 2. Budapest (Hungary)—History—Fiction. 3. Hippopotamuses—Fiction. 4. Family life—Fiction.]
I. Knutson, Barbara, ill. II. Title.
PZ7.M36825Han 2009   Fic - dc21 2008943537
ISBN-13: 978-1-9309000-40-0

Read more about our Classic Books for Children at
www.PurpleHousePress.com

Printed in China
1 2 3 4 5 6 7 8 9 10
First Edition

When I was a child, Sunday was my favorite day. Papa would wake up rested, after working all week at the paprika mill outside of town. For six days, summer and winter, he would pull heavy bags of dried peppers off the farmers' carts and haul them into the gaping mouth of the paprika factory, where they were ground into a fine spice. Papa used to say that the mouth of that factory was the only thing that was harder to feed than the mouths of his three children.

But that was on the six days during the week. On the seventh day, on Sunday, Papa could sleep until the sun woke him up. We would wait for him to come into the kitchen, dressed in his suit and his red bow tie and the gold cufflinks his grandfather had given to him when he got married.

"Well, well," he would say, trying to look stern. "I suppose I shall have no peace today. I suppose I shall have to wait to sit by the fire and drink your mother's good coffee. Your faces tell me you want to go out today."

We had been holding our breath, hoping Papa would say that. We had traveled all over Budapest, and sometimes to villages in the country, on these Sunday outings with Papa and Mama, and each of us had a special statue or building or park. I loved the carved stone lions guarding the bridge over the Danube River. My sister begged to go to the baths at the Gellert Hotel, and see the painted tiles, and feel the steam rising from the water that bubbled up from the ground.

My older brother, Gabor, who had pocket money, would run across the street from the baths to the market, where the farmers brought their eggs and tomatoes and chickens. He would soon be lost in the maze of cheese stalls and spice counters, but he always came out with candy for us all.

There was one place that
was a favorite for all of us, but
we never asked Papa to take us
there because it cost money.
We knew that when there were
extra forints after buying
Mama's sugar and butter, and
the cloth for new pants, and
new shoes for whichever one
of us had grown too much,
Papa would stand in the
kitchen, and put his hand
in his pocket, and jingle his
coins, and smile a big smile.
Then we knew it was a
zoo Sunday.

The zoo in our town was down a big hill and across the river from where we lived. Papa would lift Eva onto his shoulders and clasp my hand in his, and with Gabor running ahead, we would walk down the hill and over the river into the city of Pest.

Coming home, we could take the cog train that groaned its way up the hill, but going down was a game of chase, of hide-and-seek, and, always, of Papa's riddles.

"Little Tibor," he would ask me. "Those favorite lions of yours on the Lanchid Bridge. Tell me, what is missing from the lions who guard the bridge of Lanchid?"

I knew the answer. I knew the tongues were what was missing, but I always let Papa tell me, and we would listen to his hearty laugh.

Soon we would reach the zoo. The balloon men and
ice cream ladies lined the street in front of the entrance.
"Hurry, hurry," one of them would shout. "It is feeding
time for Hanna."

Hanna was a hippopotamus. Our city was famous for its hippos. They loved the warm springs that came naturally out of the ground, and they grew fat and healthy and had many babies that were sent to zoos all over the world.

Our city had built them a beautiful house in the zoo. It looked like a miniature palace, with copper domes and a large pool in front, and separate rooms with pools on the inside. Trees and flowers were planted around the hippo house, and the water was always kept clean.

Hanna was a special hippo. She liked being in the outside pool, close to the people. She often slept with one eye open, hoping that she would see the cart loaded with grass and hay creaking down the curved path. While the other hippos rested, she would get up just when the cart reached the giraffe house, next door. Hanna was the only hippo who was ready, mouth open, when the zookeeper had his first pitchfork full of hay poised in midair.

She would keep her mouth open until the keeper could get no more hay in, then, as fast as a hippo can, she would close her mouth. In a flash, it seemed, her mouth was open again, and all the hay was gone. The crowd would laugh, Papa loudest of all. That was one riddle even he could not figure out.

One winter, the river between the twin towns of Buda and Pest froze. It was a big river, and the winter had to be very cold for so much water to freeze. But no one talked about it much, as something much more important was happening to us. There was a war going on, all over our part of Europe, and beyond. There were now soldiers in our town, on the banks of the river, and the soldiers on either side were fighting each other.

The people would shake their heads, go to their work, then come home and stay inside. Papa no longer took us out on Sundays. We sat by the hearth and studied our lessons and mended our worn clothing, and listened to the radio, hoping for better news. But the soldiers stayed, and the days grew colder. Our meat ran out, then our potatoes. Papa would come home with only a few onions and carrots from the market, and with these vegetables and sometimes with some thin chickens our neighbors gave us, Mama always managed to stretch our soup pot.

We were so busy thinking of our own hollow stomachs that Papa's news came as a surprise. "The animals in the zoo are hungry, too," he said. "I heard that because of the soldiers no food is coming into the town, and the animals need more food when winters are this cold." We thought of Hanna, and of her wide grin, and of how much hay her mouth could hold. We thought of her baby, born that summer, and of all of our famous hippos in the zoo. We went to bed that night feeling helpless and sad.

In the morning, Papa was in the kitchen, in his suit. His hands were in his pockets, and he had a big smile on his face. "We are going to the zoo," he said, "but not for fun. We are going to save the zoo today. If you children get dressed and come with me, I will show you how."

We scrambled to our rooms and in no time were back in the kitchen. Mama wrapped mufflers around our necks. The way she looked, we knew she and Papa had stayed up late thinking of a plan to save the hippos, and that it was a good one. On the way out of our house, Papa picked up our straw doormat and an old pair of straw slippers. Gabor, Eva, and I whispered together, but we knew Papa would share his secret only when he was ready.

On the way to the zoo, Papa told us what he and Mama had planned. "We are going to the zookeeper the first thing," he said. "And we will take him to the hippo house to show him the plan will work."

When we got to the hippo house, we could see a frozen pond and bare trees around it. The hippos were huddled inside for warmth and shelter from the wind. Hanna no longer looked our way, no longer slept with one eye open. We could hardly tell which hippo she was.

Papa walked up to the hunched animals and gently put the straw mat under the nose of one. The hippo moved but did not eat. So Papa got a pitchfork and broke the mat up and put the pieces of the old mat on the end of the fork. Then Papa offered our tattered mat to the hippo. The old hippo raised himself up and opened his mouth, and the mat was gone in a twinkling. "Well done," said the zookeeper. "Well done."

After that day, on cold nights and on gray mornings, in mist and in fog and in snow, an old cart pulled by an older horse traveled the streets of Buda and Pest. "Feed the hippos, straw for the hippos," the driver's voice echoed through the streets.

The people of my town ran out of their doors and piled their old straw mats and slippers and hats onto the cart. The cart was filled time and again, and the old horse faithfully pulled each load to Hanna and the other hippos at the zoo. By the end of the winter, the people of Budapest had given nine thousand hats and mats and slippers to the hippos. The hippos did not grow fat, but the straw kept them alive through that cold and frightening winter.

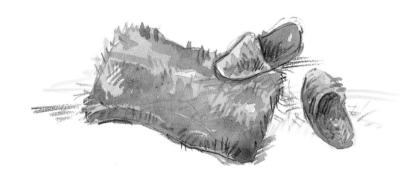

One of the most wonderful things about this book was that Barbara Knutson illustrated it. We must have been having the same vision, peering into our imaginations the same way, during our solitary sojourns of writing and illustrating. My images, rich in emotion but misty in outline, were caught by Barbara, and with her immense talent, committed to paper.

Barbara's husband, Chris Jensen, was the model for the father. "Dad," he says, "is all me but with dark hair and a mustache as I was blond at the time. I remember the pitchfork in the hay pose was actually a snow shovel in a pile of laundry." Chris goes on to say, "...my hands, mouth, arms, legs are attached to various illustrations (of Barbara's) all over the world...other family members and friends are roughly the main characters and the people outside the zoo. Barb loved hidden treasures."

Barbara's art for Hanna was lost for over a decade. It had slipped behind an editor's desk in 1992. Chris received an excited phone call in 2005 that it had been discovered, still in its sealed package. Chris opened it on Barbara's birthday. It was all there, except for the cover art. A second call to the publisher revealed that the cover to the book was on the art director's wall, and had been for fifteen years. Chris quickly sent it down to Purple House Press, again on Barbara's birthday. "The experience of finding the original art has been an undertaking of almost spiritual nature," said Chris.

For this collaboration, I am grateful. And for you, the reader, thank you for taking Hanna into your homes and your hearts. And thank you to Jill Morgan and Ray Sanders of Purple House Press for keeping her alive.

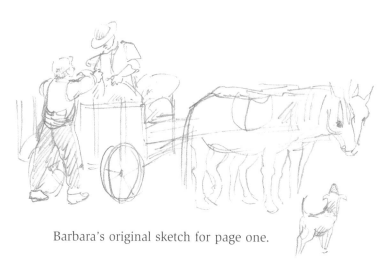

Barbara's original sketch for page one.